Karl

by **Ginger Simms**

Illustrations by
Misun Chung and Sein Park

Epigraph Books
Rhinebeck, NY

ISBN 978-1-954744-18-9

Epigraph Books
22 East Market Street, Suite 304
Rhinebeck, NY 12572
(845) 876-4861
epigraphps.com

Once upon a time there was a Mommy bear.

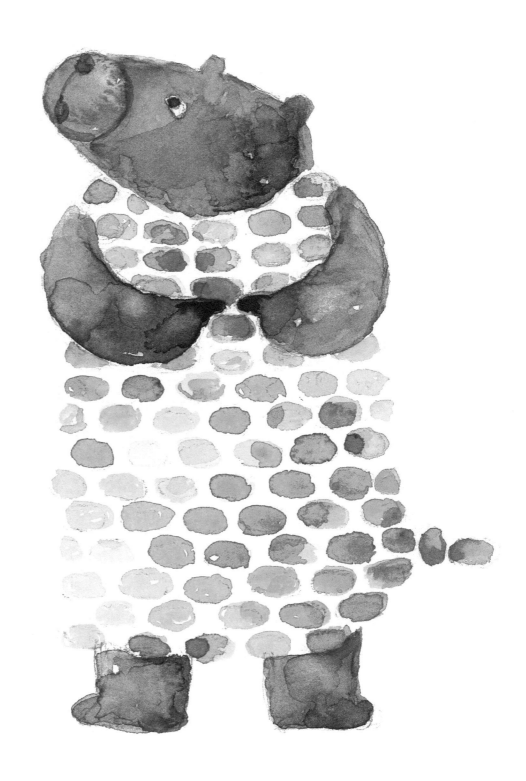

Mommy bear did not want any pets in the house because…

…she already had two little rascal cubs to look after.

But one day, Daddy bear came home with Karl.

Karl was a majestic unicorn with a rainbow mane and skin as soft as an angel's butt.

The cubs immediately took a liking to Karl.

But Mommy bear kept her distance.

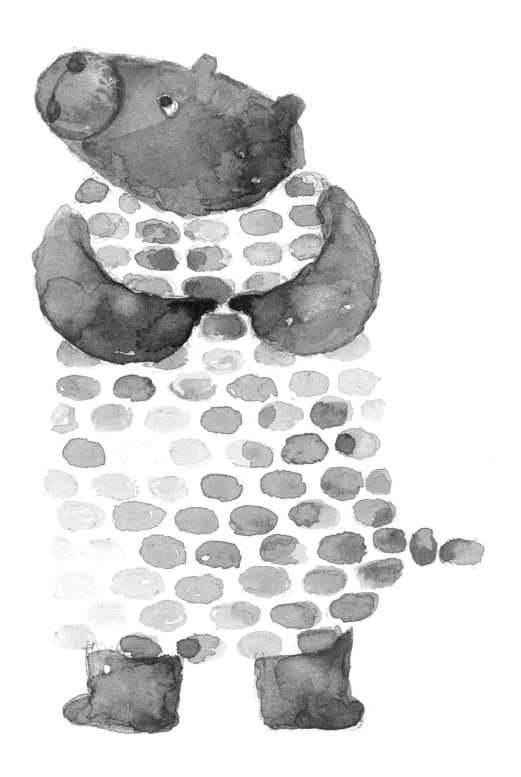

She said that she never got along well with other mammals and didn't know how to take care of Karl.

But everyone knew that she was really just afraid of getting too attached, an understandable fear given that Karl was such a lovable creature.

Mommy bear was very persistent.

Then one day school was canceled because all of the teachers spontaneously decided to go on an early hibernation.

The cubs were jumping on their beds, laughing the day away, when they heard the creak of Karl's hand-crafted stable door open.

They rushed to the windows and peeked
through the blinds.

Their little scruffy chins dropped to the floor as they saw none other than Mommy bear entering Karl's lair.

They watched with much befuddlement and much happiness as Mommy bear spent hours braiding Karl's rainbow mane and feeding him glitter cubes.

As much as they wanted to shout out to the world and share the news with Daddy bear, the cubs decided it was best to keep it on the down low so that Mommy bear could continue building her relationship with Karl without everyone watching over her.

That night, Mommy bear tucked her cubs into bed and sang them good night songs until she heard their little cub snores.

Before she left the room, she whispered into the air, "I think I'm starting to like Karl a very little bit."

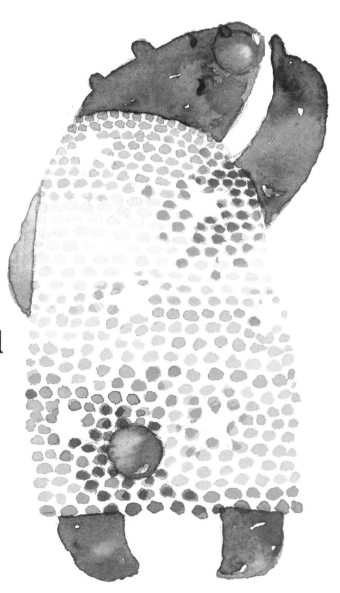

The cubs then drifted off into the most blissful dreamland and everyone lived happily ever after.

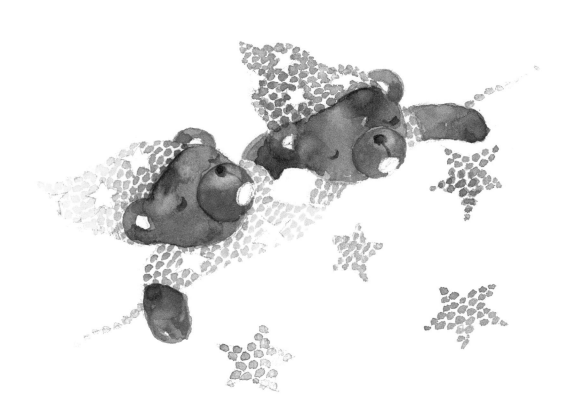

Until 3 a.m. the next morning…

...when Karl let out the hugest fart in the world!

And the smell of candy canes and melted caramel drifted into the house and everyone had to get up and eat a snack because it made them hungry.

NORTH CAROLINA
OUTWARD BOUND SCHOOL

All proceeds from the sale of this book support the Ginger Simms Leadership Fund at Outward Bound.

The fund provides scholarships to encourage, train and empower highly-motivated young women.

details & donations: www.ncobs.org/ginger-simms

Illustrations by Misun Chung & Sein Park
*Misun Chung is an artist and jewelry designer.
She and her son Sein reside in Great Neck, NY.*

With love and appreciation to the Gilmartin-Lings:
Charmian, Bob, Dorian, and especially Gemma...
(who inspired this project in more ways than one).

Ginger Simms

The light of a good character surpasseth the light of the sun.

Bahá'í proverb

CPSIA information can be obtained
at www.ICGtesting.com
Printed in the USA
BVHW022209160422
634529BV00005B/134